For everyone who is compelled to create,
no matter what. —S.B.

For Sarah Jane and Julia, my artistic soul mates,
who continue to inspire me to create. —M.C.

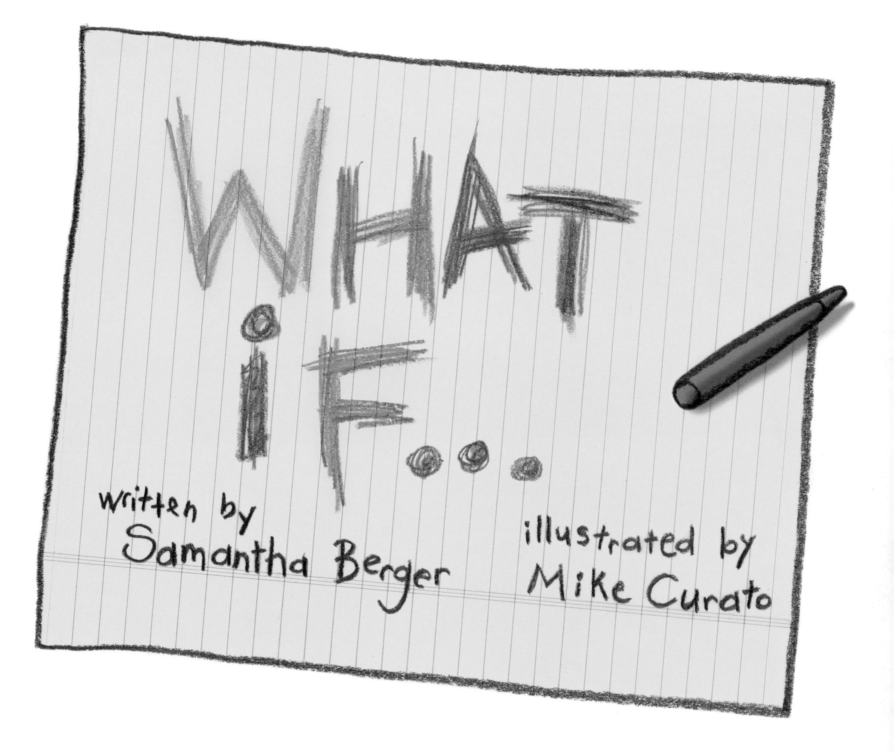

WHAT iF...

written by
Samantha Berger

illustrated by
Mike Curato

LITTLE, BROWN AND COMPANY
NEW YORK   BOSTON

With a pencil and paper, I write and draw art
to create many stories that come from my heart.

But what if that pencil
one day disappeared?

I'd fold up the paper
till stories appeared.

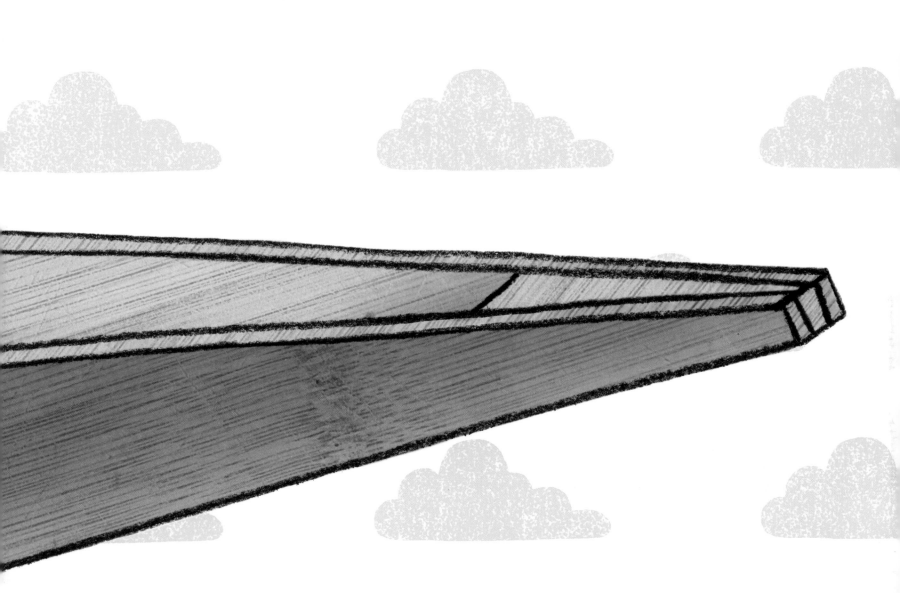

And what if that paper was no longer there?
I'd chisel the table and then carve the chair.

And what if there wasn't
a chair here at all?
I'd chip and I'd peel
at the paint on the wall.

And what if there wasn't
a wall anymore?
I might build a story
from boards in the floor.

7...
6...
5...
4...

Without any floor,
I could still use the land
and sketch out a tale
in the dirt with my hand.

I could still shape the leaves.

I could still sculpt the snow.

I could still plant the flowers
and make kingdoms grow.

Without any land, I would still use the light—

invent shadow stories the sun would ignite.

If there was no light,
I would still use my voice
to sing out my stories—
to chant and rejoice!

I'd still have my body to twist and to bend—
to dance out my stories, beginning to end.

If I had nothing,

but still had my mind…

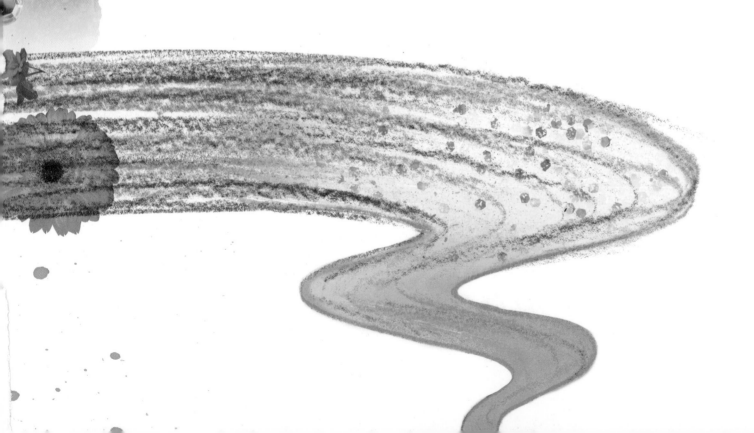

There'd always be stories to seek and to find.

If I know nothing but one bit of fate…

As long as I live, I will always create.

As long as I live…

I will always create.

A NOTE FROM THE AUTHOR AND ARTIST

I WROTE THE FIRST DRAFT of this book after a flood forced me to evacuate my apartment with nothing but my dog and my sketchbook. I was right in the middle of a big creative project, and I was making a new piece every day. After the flood hit, I had nothing to work with at all: no paints, no brushes, no markers, no nothing.

It was then that I started to realize *anything* could be used as an art supply—the pinecones on the trees, the paper in the recycling bin, the kibble in my dog's dish—and I used them all! When I understood that *everything* could be used to express myself, it made me see the world in a new way.

It also made me see *myself* in a new way. Throughout my life, I have always wondered how some people have found a way to create under the most difficult circumstances. Now that I see I am also someone compelled to create, I know I will always find a way. I wrote this story for them, and for you, and for all of us who *have* to. —*Samantha*

I MET SAMANTHA right about the time her apartment flooded.

When we first talked about illustrating this book, I thought about how she was using found objects to continue to create art. That inspired me to use many different things to make the illustrations in this book. I used traditional art supplies like pencil, paper, and ink. But I also added objects found in nature, like seashells, moss, and dirt. I even used stuff from around the house, like brown paper bags, a wooden cutting board, and marbles. You can create with just about anything, but the most important art supplies you have are your mind and your heart. When you use them both, everything you make will be beautiful. —*Mike*

AFTER MEETING at a picture book party, and singing an Ella Fitzgerald and Louis Armstrong duet, we became the best of buds. During the making of this book, we wrote and drew together, we folded origami together (*some* tried harder than others), we sang a lot of songs, danced a lot of dances, and laughed a lot of laughs together. We worked on it and worked on it. And now, together, we hope you like it. ❤ Us

ACKNOWLEDGMENTS

SAMANTHA would like to acknowledge Alva Chang, Steven Shin, and Scooby, who let her stay at their house for three months after the flood. And Kirsten, Antonia, and Oscar for hosting her in Hudson. True friends indeed.

MIKE would like to acknowledge Timeca Briggs for her thoughtful input, Ruth Chan for lending her skyline photo to his collage (and for being a good friend), and Pidge Pidge for photographs of their beautiful woven fabrics that appear in this book.